Jungle School

Elizabeth Laird • Roz Davison • David Sim

EGMONT

We bring stories to life

Book Band: Green

First published in Great Britain 2006
by Egmont UK Ltd.
The Yellow Building, 1 Nicholas Road, London W11 4AN
Text copyright © Elizabeth Laird and Roz Davison 2006
Illustrations copyright © David Sim 2006
The authors and illustrator have asserted their moral rights.
ISBN 978 1 4052 1919 8
10 9 8 7 6 5 4 3 2 1
A CIP catalogue record for this title is available from the British Library.
Printed in Singapore
43610/10

EGMONT LUCKY COIN

Our story began over a century ago, when seventeen-year-old Egmont Harald Petersen found a coin in the street.

He was on his way to buy a flyswatter, a small hand-operated printing machine that he then set up in his tiny apartment.

The coin brought him such good luck that today Egmont has offices in over 30 countries around the world. And that lucky coin is still kept at the company's head offices in Denmark.

FIRST DAY AT SCHOOL

WELL DONE, JANI!

YOU CHEEKY MONKEY!

Green Bananas

For Amy, Olivia and Phoebe Jones

R. D.

For Rachel

D. S.

FIRST DAY AT SCHOOL

It was Jani's first day at Jungle
School.

All the little monkeys stared at her.

She didn't like being the new girl.

'Come on, Jani,' said Miss Mango.

'Don't be shy.'

One monkey waved at Jani.

'Hi,' he said. 'I'm Abe.'

Another monkey smiled at her.

'Hello,' she said. 'I'm Olivia.'

Jani went to sit at their table.

'Why has your chair got wheels?'

asked Abe.

'Because my legs aren't very strong,'

said Jani.

'How do you make it move?'

said Olivia.

'With my hands,' said Jani.

'Like this.'

All the other monkeys just stared.

'Do you mind people staring at you?' said Olivia.

'New girls always get stared at,' said Jani. 'Sometimes it's OK and I feel like a filmstar.'

'But sometimes it's rude, and I don't like it at all.'

'Playtime!' said Miss Mango.

The little monkeys all began to skip
and run about.

'I'll hold the skipping rope,' said Jani.

'I'll hold the other end,' said Olivia.

I'm tired.

The skipping rope went round and round and round.

Me Tarzan!

Jani wasn't tired. Her arms were very strong.

Abe ran up to her.

'Can I have a go on your
wheelchair?' he said.

'OK,' said Jani.

'Can I?' asked Olivia.

'Yes!' said Jani.

The other monkeys stared and

jumped up and down. They shouted,

'Me too! Me too!'

17

'I like jungle school,' said Jani.

'I don't feel like a new girl any more.'

Later it was P.E.

'Today we're going to pick things up

with our tails,' said Miss Mango.

'Watch me, everyone.'

21

The monkeys stood in a line.

It was difficult for Jani to reach the

hoop with her tail.

Then she had an idea.

'Can I do my own PE?' she asked.

'Sure, Jani,' said Miss Mango.

Jani raced her chair up and down.

She went round and round in circles.

All the other monkeys stopped what

they were doing and watched her.

Jani didn't stop until she was quite
puffed out.

'I really like your chair,' said Olivia.

'So do I,' said Jani. 'It's what makes
me me.'

'What do you mean?' asked Olivia and Abe.

'Well, we are all different, aren't we?' said Jani.

'Some of us are short, and some of us are tall.'

29

'Some of us are good at swatting

flies. And some of us aren't.'

'And some people have got chairs

with wheels. Like you!' said Abe.

'Come on, monkeys!' said Miss

Mango. 'Catch!' And she threw some

balls up high.

Abe caught a green one.

Olivia caught a pink one.

But Jani caught a yellow one AND

a blue one.

'Well done, Jani,' said Miss Mango.

And all the other monkeys clapped.

YOU CHEEKY MONKEY!

Miss Mango got out the dressing

up box.

36

Jani was very happy.

She liked dressing up.

The other monkeys all ran to the box. They began to pull things out.

Jani couldn't decide what to wear.

'I could be a princess,' she thought.

'Or a cowgirl. Or what about a

pirate!'

41

'Stand back, all of you,' said Miss Mango. 'Now, what do you want, Abe?'

'The wizard's cloak,' said Abe.

'I want to be a rabbit,' said Olivia.

'And what do you want, Jani?' said

Miss Mango.

'Please can I have the pirate hat?'

said Jani.

Jani looked great in the pirate hat.

'Which ribbon shall my parrot

wear?' she said.

'Black's cool,' said Abe. 'Like my cloak.'

'Pink's pretty,' said Olivia.

'Oh no,' said Jani. 'I like yellow.'

Everyone was dressed up now.

They all began to play.

Abe tried to put a spell on Jani.

He wanted to turn her into a frog.

Olivia pretended to be Jani's pet rabbit. Jani stroked her ears.

Miss Mango took out her camera.

'Well done, monkeys,' she said.

'Smile, please, everyone!'

But what is Jani up to?

Oh! She's dressed up just like

Miss Mango!

'You cheeky monkey!' said

Miss Mango, laughing.